The
Railway
Runaways

When their cross governess punishes James and Jenny Murray by sending them to bed in the middle of the day, the eight-year-old twins hatch a daring plan for an adventure. The young Queen Victoria has come to Edinburgh on a visit, and Jenny is determined to see her. James, meanwhile, is longing for a trip on the wonderful, horse-drawn Innocent Railway.

So the twins, against all rules and without permission, slip out of the house for an exciting journey to see the Queen. They have a glorious ride in the open railway carriage, pulled by great, strong horses, with a thrilling passage through a long and frightening tunnel. They meet all sorts of extra-ordinary people, and find two new friends of their own age. And, of course, they see the Queen.

It is a delicious day, full of discoveries and comical mishaps, and well worth the awful consequences they expect to suffer when they get home.

The Innocent Railway really existed, an all-but-forgotten precursor of the great steam-engines, and Kathleen Fidler brings it, and the people who used it, vividly to life.

The Railway Runaways

Kathleen Fidler

Illustrated by Terry Gabbey

Blackie: Glasgow and London

ISBN   0   216   90296 7

Blackie & Son Limited
Bishopbriggs, Glasgow G64 2NZ
450/452 Edgware Road, London W2 1EG

Printed in Great Britain by
The Anchor Press Ltd, Tiptree, Essex

Contents

A Note to the Reader

The twins, James and Jenny Murray, lived at Gibraltar House, which faced Edinburgh's mountain, Arthur's Seat. The back of their home overlooked the railway yard of St Leonard's, the starting-point of the Edinburgh to Dalkeith railway. In 1842 this was a different railway from those of today. The coaches and trucks ran on rails but they were pulled by *horses*, not by steam locomotives, for steam railways had not then reached Edinburgh. It was a friendly kind of railway, for the drivers would stop anywhere along the route to pick up passengers. Edinburgh people called it the "Innocent Railway", because in all the years it ran, from 1831 to 1845, it never had a single accident.

When Queen Victoria visited Dalkeith Palace in 1842 hundreds of people travelled on the Innocent Railway to see her.

Gibraltar House still stands, looking towards Arthur's Seat. Behind it, the St Leonard's Railway Yard is now a big car park. The tunnel is still there, too, but it is boarded up and closed now. You can still see Dalkeith

Palace and the gates that open on to the wide Market Place at Dalkeith, where James and Jenny waited with their new friends to see the Queen, and where new adventures befell them.

Kathleen Fidler

For James H. Goldie
and Catriona M. Goldie

The Innocent Railway

The twins, James and Jenny Murray, stood on the steps of Gibraltar House with Miss Greig who came every day to teach them reading, writing and simple arithmetic and to take them for a walk. They were just eight years old.

"Today," Miss Greig said firmly, "we are going to see the Queen."

Jenny clapped her hands in excitement, but James looked disappointed. "I'd rather go and see the horses on the railway," he told Miss Greig.

Miss Greig looked shocked. "You can see the horses any day but Queen Victoria might not come again to Edinburgh for years and years."

"I *like* the horses and the railway and the tunnel," James said stubbornly. "I don't want to see the Queen."

"Oh, you dreadful boy!" Miss Greig cried. "You'll do as you are told or I shall have to tell your mamma and papa and you'll be whipped."

"Oh, come on, James! Perhaps we can go and see the horses and the railway tomorrow," Jenny coaxed him.

Miss Greig jammed their hats on their heads. "Come along! We shall have to hurry or we shall miss the Queen." She hustled them out of the house and along the road.

It was the first day of September in the year 1842. Queen Victoria was to land at the port of Leith on her way through Edinburgh to stay at Dalkeith Palace. She was expected to pass close by Holyrood Palace, which was not far away from Gibraltar House.

Gibraltar House was the biggest and most important-looking house in the whole street of St Leonard's Bank. Across the valley it faced Edinburgh's mountain, Arthur's Seat. The back of the house looked down upon the great maze of rails and coal-yards. This was the starting-point of the Edinburgh to Dalkeith railway, called by the people who travelled on it "The Innocent Railway". It was built before the days of steam trains in Edinburgh and its coaches and trucks were pulled along the rails by teams of horses. The twins loved to look out of the back windows of Gibraltar House and watch all the bustle of the railway yard below. When Miss Greig was in a very good humour she would sometimes take them right into the railway yard to have a closer look at the horses and the entrance to the mysterious tunnel that ran under the lower part of craggy Arthur's Seat. On this particular day, however,

Miss Greig was bent on seeing Queen Victoria. She took a hand of each of the twins and rushed them along. "We'll have to run if we are to see the Queen near Abbeyhill."

"But Papa said a cannon would be fired when the Queen landed," Jenny gasped, already out of breath. "We haven't heard a cannon yet. There'll be heaps of time."

That is what everyone thought: there would be plenty of time to see the Queen. The cannon had not been fired, so the Queen could not have landed yet from her ship. But when James and Jenny and Miss Greig reached London Road they found the crowds were already breaking up and moving away. The people wore a sad disappointed look. Many were running in the opposite direction.

"Where's the Queen? Isn't she coming?" Miss Greig demanded of a woman passing them.

"The Queen? She's *gone*!"

"Gone! But there was to be a cannon fired. . . ."

"Ay, that's what everyone thought but someone forgot to fire it! She's past and away to Dalkeith Palace with only a two-three people to give her a cheer. She'll be almost half-way there by now."

"Then where are all these people running?"

"To get on the railway at St Leonard's to go to

Dalkeith. They think there might be a chance of seeing her there."

"Oh, my! Oh, my!" Miss Greig lamented.

Jenny began to sob. "Shan't we see the Queen at all?"

"Not unless you go to Dalkeith and even then you might have to wait till tomorrow. The Queen will be behind the gates of Dalkeith Palace before you could get there." The woman turned away.

"Can't we go to Dalkeith?" Jenny pleaded with Miss Greig.

"No, you can't!" Miss Greig said crossly. "I never heard such nonsense."

"I wish we'd never bothered about the Queen. We should have gone to the railway yard instead. At least we'd have seen the *horses* there," James told Miss Greig glumly.

Miss Greig gave him a slap. "Another word from you, James, you horrid little boy, and you shall never go to see the railway horses again! Back home, now!"

The two children trailed after Miss Greig. Every now and then James got behind her and pulled a face at her back. Jenny got behind too and joined in the face-pulling. Unluckily Miss Greig turned round and caught them both at it.

"You rude children! To bed you go, the minute we get home!" She pushed them in front of her till they reached Gibraltar House, then up the two flights of stairs to each of the attic bedrooms where they slept, then slammed and locked the doors on them.

"There you stay till tea-time and no dinner!" she said grimly and went downstairs.

It was no use banging on the doors and shouting. They knew Miss Greig would not let them out. Besides, Papa had said that Mamma had not to be disturbed because she was not well, so each of the twins went to the window and looked out. Jenny slept in the front attic that looked upon Arthur's Seat, while James slept in the back attic that looked down over the railway yard.

Jenny looked at her much loved mountain, at the long green sweep of it like the shape of a lion lying down. Below the house a railing enclosed a tiny belt of trees and beyond that was the Queen's Park with its pathways among the green turf, rising to the red craggy rocks round the base of the mountain. Away round the curve of the lion's flank was Duddingston Loch. Sometimes Miss Greig took them there to feed crusts of bread to the ducks. Jenny sighed. When Miss Greig was cross it often lasted for days. It would be no use suggesting going to the loch tomorrow.

James liked the view from his window far better than the one from Jenny's. There was so much more going on there in the railway yard below. The rails spread out like a fan and each line ended at a little stone building with a weighing machine for the coal which was brought in trucks from the coal-mines around Dalkeith. One set of rails went to the saw-mill just at the end of their street, and trunks of trees were brought there to be sawn up. When James leaned out of the window he could see all the twenty sidings and the coal carts waiting by them to be loaded up from the trains. That was why the railway had been built in the first place, to haul coal from the coalfields right into the heart of Edinburgh. James stretched his head out a little further and looked to the left till he could see the entrance to the tunnel under "Samson's Ribs". The horses were there waiting to take over the coaches and trucks as they came up from the tunnel. Just beside the tunnel was an engine, worked by steam, but it was not one which *moved* along the rails. It wound up the long steel ropes that hauled the trucks uphill through the tunnel. At the same time it let down the tunnel the trucks which were going to Dalkeith. In 1842 there were no steam locomotives pulling trains out of Edinburgh. At each end of the tunnel horses stood waiting to be yoked to the trains.

James loved the horses. Great strong horses they were with feet as big as soup plates. When James stood beside them he could only reach up to their chests. For all they were so big they were good-tempered and obedient. Once, when Miss Greig was in a good mood, she took the twins down to the "station", a cobbled pavement beside the manager's house, where the people climbed up on to the passenger coaches. Some of the coaches had a roof to keep the rain off the passengers; some were just like open trucks with benches across them. The driver sat in front of an open truck. He collected the fares too. As each train filled up, the horses drew it on the rails across the yard to the entrance to the tunnel. James looked eagerly at the horses as he stood by Miss Greig. The train driver noticed him.

"Like to go up on a horse, laddie?" he asked.

James was speechless with delight and could only nod his head. He felt himself hoisted up in strong arms.

"Put your legs astride," the driver told him.

James found himself seated on the broad back. His legs were so short that they stuck out on each side from the horse. His eyes shone with delight as he stroked the horse's neck.

"Would you like to ride him as far as the tunnel? I'll walk alongside you so you canna fall off," the good-natured driver offered, but Miss Greig would have none of it.

"Oh, no! Oh, no!" she cried. "I can't allow it. It's not safe. Lift him down at once. Besides, the child might get fleas from the horse."

"I'll have ye know there are no fleas on *my* horses, mistress," the driver exclaimed, very annoyed, but he lifted James down. James was almost in tears. Why did Miss Greig always have to say "No!" and spoil things?

"Never mind, laddie! One day you'll maybe drive the horses yourself," the driver said, sorry for him.

"If I can't ride the horse, please can we go and look at the steam-engine at the end of the tunnel?" James begged Miss Greig. She hesitated.

"Go on, mistress. Let the wee lad have his bit of pleasure," the driver urged her. "You'll find no fleas on the engine, certain sure!"

"Rude man!" Miss Greig exclaimed. She seized the twins by the hands and hurried them along the cobbled road. She was so angry that she was almost at the tunnel entrance before she realized where they were. Anything to get away from that horrible train driver!

The steam-engine was snorting like a giant in a deep sleep as the pistons went gliding smoothly up and down and the long chain cables clanked and groaned as they wound and unwound round the two drums. James watched with large eyes. He pulled his hand out of Miss Greig's. "There'll be a train coming up the tunnel!" he cried and ran towards the entrance. Before he had taken more than a step or two Miss Greig spun him round by the shoulder.

"You naughty boy! How dare you let go my hand to go down that tunnel!"

"But I wasn't going *down*. I was only going nearer so I could see the train coming out," James protested, but Miss Greig pulled him backwards.

"We'll not stay here a minute longer. I never know what you'll be up to next. First the horse and now the tunnel! And your sister has got her clean dress covered in smuts from the coal-dust that's blowing round!"

Jenny set up a howl, partly because of her dress and partly because she was sorry for James. "I wanted to see the tunnel too," she cried. She always backed up James in everything he wanted to do.

Miss Greig gripped them both so tightly by the wrists that it hurt and tugged them towards the entrance gates to the railway.

"Someday . . . someday I shall go on that train and I shall go down that tunnel and no one will stop me!" James told Miss Greig fiercely. "I'll go all the way to Dalkeith!" he added defiantly.

"No more of this nonsense! Right this minute you

are coming home and it will be a long time before you get me to come to this horrible dirty railway yard again, if ever!" she threatened.

As she pulled him along James threw a backward glance at the tunnel entrance. The coaches were coming out one by one with their loads of passengers, followed by the coal trucks. Miss Greig gave an angry tug at his wrist and he almost fell. At that moment James hated Miss Greig more than ever.

James was remembering all that had happened on this visit as he leaned out of the attic window. He watched the bustle of horses and trains and coal carts below.

"Miss Greig will be so vexed we haven't seen Queen Victoria and so angry because we pulled faces at her that she will *never* take us to look at the railway again," he muttered in despair. He watched the train filling up. "And all those people are going to Dalkeith to see the Queen!"

It was just then that James had his big idea!

2

James Has an Idea

Between James's attic room and Jenny's there was a door. It had been locked long ago, before the Murrays had come to live at Gibraltar House, then the key had been lost and no one had ever bothered to find it and unlock the door. When the twins were in disgrace and sent to their rooms they found they could talk to each other in whispers through the keyhole. James left his window and whistled through the keyhole to call Jenny.

Jenny was at her window too. She had been gazing at the red-brown crags and great green hill of Arthur's Seat and wishing she could fly like a bird to the top. Perhaps tomorrow Miss Greig would be less cross and she would let them climb part way up the hill? But then Miss Greig always said it made her out of breath and it was too windy higher up. Once Papa had taken them right to the top by the pathway near Duddingston Loch. Jenny remembered how she could see the shining blue waters of the Firth of Forth and the hills of Fife to the north and when she turned round, all Edinburgh was spread out like a toy-town at her feet. Mr Murray was a busy man and he only had time on a holiday to take the children for an outing. When Jenny had begged him to take them up Arthur's Seat again he had stroked her hair and said, "Next May Day I'll take you up there to see the sun rise and you can wash your face in the magic mountain dew and then you'll be beautiful for ever."

Jenny longed for May Day to come round, but it was only the first day of September and May Day seemed a terribly long time away. Jenny felt sad.

"We didn't see Queen Victoria and we got all hot and tired and Miss Greig was in a terrible temper. And now we've had no dinner either! And I did want to see what the Queen was like. I wonder if she had her crown on her head and a red velvet cloak round her shoulders?" she thought.

Just then she heard James whistle through the key-hole. When she bent down to it James whispered loudly, "I've got an idea."

"Oh!" Jenny gave a little groan. When James had one of his ideas it always seemed to get them into trouble.

"Don't you want to hear it?" James asked.

"Well . . . yes. What is it?"

"You want to see Queen Victoria, don't you?"

"Yes, but what's the use now?"

"And I want to go on the Innocent Railway. That woman this morning told Miss Greig that people would be able to see the Queen at Dalkeith. Let's go and see the Queen there."

"How can we? Pigs might fly! Miss Greig will never take us."

"Oh, but I mean us to go without Miss Greig!"

Jenny gave a gasp of amazement. "We can't do that!"

"Yes, we can! Now, listen! I've got a really good plan. Have you got any of your birthday money left from last week?"

"I've still got my shilling. Why?"

"I've got my shilling too. So we've got plenty of money."

"What for?"

"To pay our fares on the train, silly!"

"But I was saving up my money to buy Mamma's birthday present," Jenny objected.

"Her birthday isn't till November and we'll have plenty of time to save up again. And this will be the *only* chance for you to see the Queen," James coaxed her.

"But Miss Greig will never let us go."

"We're not going to ask her. We're just going to run away from home tomorrow."

"But Miss Greig will be with us all the morning."

"She doesn't come till nine o'clock. Maggie gives us our breakfast at a quarter to eight. We can eat our breakfast quickly and be out of the house just after eight o'clock. By the time Miss Greig comes we can be on our way to Dalkeith on the train."

"But someone will be sure to see us go through the front door and ask us where we are going."

"But we shan't go by the front door. We'll go right downstairs to the passage that opens on to the back garden. From there we can slip down the steps and out of the door at the big wall and right out on to the railway yards."

"But that door in the wall is always kept locked," Jenny reminded him.

"Yes, but I know where the key is hung. It's kept just inside the coal-cellar so that it's handy for when the coalmen bring the coal. We can lock the door behind us and I'll take the key in my pocket, so we can get in again that way."

Still Jenny hesitated.

"Oh, come on! Say you'll come."

"But they'll know we've been away," Jenny pointed out. "It'll be bread and water for a day when we get back."

"Yes, but by then you'll have seen the Queen and

I'll have been on the railway. It'll be worth it. It'll be a big adventure. Say you'll come, Jenny. I don't want to have to go by myself."

Jenny could not bear the thought of James going by himself. They always did everything together. Besides, what trouble might James get into by himself, without her? She took a deep breath. "All right! I'll come. Listen! I can hear Miss Greig coming up the stairs."

Quickly they left the keyhole. When Miss Greig opened their doors Jenny was sitting in a chair by the bed knitting a kettle-holder. James was staring through the window. Both children were very quiet.

"You can come downstairs now and do some lessons," she said. "Then, if you behave yourselves you may have your porridge for supper."

They followed Miss Greig meekly down the stairs.

"That's taught them a lesson," Miss Greig said to herself, but if she had known what the twins were planning, she wouldn't have felt so sure.

Next morning the twins did not have to be wakened. When Maggie called them they were already up and dressed. As they waited in the school-room for her to bring their porridge upstairs from the kitchen James whispered to Jenny, "Got your shilling?"

She tapped her pocket and nodded.

"Eat your porridge but put your oat-cakes in your pocket," he told her. "We may have to wait at Dalkeith a long time to see the Queen and we'll be hungry."

As soon as Maggie's back was turned they wrapped their buttered bannocks in their clean handkerchiefs and stuffed them into their pockets. When Maggie came back into the room again James asked, "Are there any more bannocks, Maggie?"

"My, you've been quick eating those!" she exclaimed, looking at the empty plate. All the same she brought them two more oat-bannocks, for she was a good-natured girl.

"We'll eat them in the back garden," James told her. "We want to play there till Miss Greig comes."

They made their way out past the kitchen door. The cook saw them going down the cellar stairs. "Where are they off to?" she asked Maggie.

"Och! They're awa' oot to play in the back garden," Maggie told her. "Poor bairns! They don't get much fun with that old sour-face of a teacher."

"Awa' you, and take the mistress her breakfast up to bed, and hold your tongue about Miss Greig," Cook snapped at her. "Ye're too impudent by far!"

James and Jenny slipped quietly along the cellar passage which opened on to the garden. James stealthily opened the door of the coal-cellar and felt with his hand behind it. The key was hanging on a nail there all right.

"Got it!" he said to Jenny. "Come on."

Out in the garden they gave a quick glance at the windows of the house to be sure that no one was watching them, then they crept down the steps into the well of the doorway. James put the key in the lock and it turned easily. A twist of the knob and the door opened. In a second they were outside and James closed the door behind them. Now they were on the other side of the big wall where no one could see them from the house. Their father had already had his breakfast and left the house and their mother, who was not well, had her breakfast in bed. Cook and Maggie would be too busy in the kitchen to bother looking out of the window. No one had seen them leave the garden.

Now they had to cross the enormous coal-yards with the ten lines of rails, to reach the station on the other side. They kept a row of trucks between them and the house, just in case anyone happened to look through a window upstairs.

The "station" was just a low cobbled pavement. People were already swarming into the coaches, for there were no tickets to buy. The driver of each train collected the money from the passengers on the way to Dalkeith. There was quite a crowd, for a number of

people had had the notion of going to Dalkeith to see the Queen. She was staying at the Duke of Buccleuch's Dalkeith Palace and it had been said she would be taking a ride in her coach through the town.

"Mix with all these people and no one will guess we're by ourselves," James told Jenny. "But keep hold of my hand so we don't lose each other."

Jenny clutched his hand tightly. She was beginning to feel a bit frightened, but James's eyes were shining.

"The adventure is really beginning," he told Jenny.

3

Journey through the Tunnel

When the twins reached the station the horses were being yoked to the train and the crowd pressed round the coaches: some coaches with covered tops; others just open trucks with rows of seats. The drivers were hurrying the people on to the trains. James and Jenny tacked themselves on to a lady with a large family of children. The lady was very flustered and the train driver helped her to lift her children aboard.

"Oh dear! Have I got everybody? Let me count them up!" she cried. "Arabella, Euphemia, William, Sarah, Charlotte." In a panic she exclaimed, "Where's Charlotte? What's happened to Charlotte?"

"You've got Charlotte in your arms, Mamma," Arabella pointed out.

"Oh, so I have! But there's one missing. Which child is it? It's Thomas. Where's Thomas? Arabella, have you seen Thomas? Mercy me! I hope he's not crawled under the train!"

Arabella pointed to the other side of the yard. "Is that Thomas over there looking at the horses on the other line?"

"Oh, wait a bit, please, driver, while I go and find my wee boy," the distracted mother begged. "I can't go without him."

"All right, missus! I'll be putting this lot on the train for you," the good-natured driver said. He was lifting William up the step when a man dressed in a check coat and breeches rushed up.

"Hi, John! Are you going to hang around St Leonard's all day? I've got business in the corn market at Dalkeith, I'd have ye mind," he barked.

"All right, Mr Henderson. We'll be off now." The driver shouted, "All aboard the train! All aboard the train!"

The lady came running back. "Can you not wait a minute, driver? I must get my wee lad."

"Sorry, missus, but I've got to start off as soon as I've got folk aboard or I'll be in trouble with the railway manager. But you'll catch up with us at the stop at the entrance to the tunnel over there. We've got to wait at the tunnel while the horses are unyoked and the cable's hitched on to the train to let it down the tunnel. It takes a minute or two. We'll not go without you, I promise."

The lady rushed across the yard to find the missing Thomas while the driver put the rest of her family aboard the first coach, an open one. "What's your name?" he asked one little girl as he lifted her up.

"Sarah Mackay," she told him shyly.

When the driver came to James and Jenny he said, "You'll be twins, I reckon?"

"Yes," said James.

"My! Your mother's got a right handful of bairns," the driver said to Arabella who was the last to get on the coach. It was only then the twins realized that the driver thought they were all part of the same big family! They giggled but said nothing as he crowded them into the same open truck with seats placed across it.

James pushed his way to the front of the truck, pulling Jenny after him. "I want to sit beside the driver and be near the horses," he said.

"Ay, you can sit beside me, laddie," the friendly driver told him.

There were all kinds of people boarding the train: sight-seers going to Dalkeith to get a glimpse of the Queen; merchants going to the Dalkeith grain market; a soldier on his way to join the Dalkeith Town Guard, a fine fellow in a red coat and brass buttons, who came and sat behind the children in the first coach too.

The two horses hauled the train over to the tunnel entrance. There they stopped of their own accord from force of habit while they were unyoked. The wire cable was hitched on to the train to let it down through the tunnel. The train waited at the entrance.

"We've got to wait here till the chap who works the engine gets the signal from the other end of the tunnel that a train is ready to come up," the driver explained to James. He looked round for the children's mother. There was Mrs Mackay, puffing and panting as she ran towards the train, pushing the whimpering Thomas in front of her.

"Take your time, missus! We're not quite ready for away yet," the driver called to her.

She bustled Thomas aboard the train. "You naughty boy! You just keep hold of Arabella's hand for the rest of the day! If you stray off again, I'll spank you, do you hear?"

"Yes, Mamma," Thomas replied meekly.

"You poor soul! You've got your hands full with all this family," the driver said pityingly. "I'll just manage to squeeze you all in. Mr Henderson, if you'll tak' that wee lad on your knee and push up a bit there'll be room for the lady."

Mr Henderson took William on his knee and made room for Mrs Mackay. She kept hold of Thomas and took Charlotte on her knee too.

Thomas looked longingly at the end of the seat next to James. "I'd like to sit next to the driver, Mamma," he begged.

"That you will not!" Mrs Mackay declared. "You've

been enough trouble already. Next thing I know, you'll be falling off the train."

"Och, missus, he'll be all right next to the other little lad. I'll keep an eye on them both," the driver offered. "Move up a bit, laddie," he said to James. Thomas was squeezed into the very narrow space.

"While we're waiting for the other train I may as well tak' your fares," the driver said. "Sixpence each to Dalkeith. Children half-price. I'll not charge you for the two that are sitting on the gentleman's knee and yours, ma'am," he told Mrs Mackay. "That'll be two shillings from you."

Mrs Mackay was still so out of breath and flustered that she could never have done the sum in her head. After a hunt for her purse she handed over two shillings to the driver. She did not know that the driver thought that James and Jenny belonged to her too and she had paid for them. When the driver did not ask them for their fares Jenny guessed what had happened.

"Oh James, the lady with all these children has paid for us too. He thinks we belong to her family," she whispered. "We must give her the money at once."

"Not *now*! Wait till we get to Dalkeith. I'll give it her then. We don't want the driver asking who we *are* with," James warned her. "Besides, we can't do it just now. We're just starting down the tunnel."

The steam engine which worked the cable drums was making thudding, thumping sounds. The driver lighted a lantern and fixed it on a hook at the front of his coach. He took his seat again beside James and sounded a post-horn. The wire cable on the drum began to unwind slowly. The cable on the opposite drum began to wind up again. Rattling and clanking the train started down the slope into the tunnel.

"Oh, Mamma! Where are we going? It's getting dark. Oh, I'm feart!" Sarah cried, and the other children, all except Arabella, set up a wail too.

"Och, you bairns! It's only a tunnel!" Mrs Mackay cried. William began to squirm on Mr Henderson's knee and to wail too.

"Come now, laddie! The tunnel's just a road dug out under Arthur's Seat, the big hill, ye ken, to let the train through. Watch now, and you'll see the light appear at the end of it, the way we're going," Mr Henderson comforted him.

James, sitting near the driver, with Thomas between them, took a deep breath. "This really is a big adventure," he whispered to Jenny at his side. Jenny held on rather tightly to his arm. She was not sure that she wasn't a bit frightened at the rattling echoing noises and the darkness. James opened his eyes wide to try to see through the murk of the tunnel. The feeble light from the driver's lantern now and again was reflected on the sides of the tunnel, glistening with damp. A silence fell upon the passengers. No one seemed to want to talk. The noise in the tunnel suddenly increased: the wire cable clanked louder and rattling sounds came towards them and echoed in the roof. A faint yellow light rushed upwards to meet them.

"Oh, what's that?" Jenny cried, clutching at James's arm.

The driver heard her above the increasing din. "Don't be feart, lassie. It's just the driver's lamp on the other train that you can see."

"The other train?"

"Ay. As we go down, the other train comes up."

"But won't it bang into us?"

"No, no. It's a double line through the tunnel. Here it comes!"

The other train drew level with them on the opposite line. "Hi, there, Harry!" their driver shouted above all the clanking noises.

"Hullo, John!" the other driver greeted him. "Busy day today!"

In the dim light cast by the lamps the passengers on the opposite train appeared like ghostly shadows to Jenny. They did not look like people at all. She held her breath and shut her eyes. When she opened them again,

the clanking noise was less and the other train had passed them on its way up to the daylight and St Leonard's.

James let go a great breath too. "That was terribly exciting, like a ghost train passing us."

Jenny shivered. "I'm glad it's gone."

"It's all right, Jenny. All the trains pass each other in the tunnel. It means we're more than half-way through, now." James gave her comfort.

"Watch in front of you," the driver told them. "You'll soon see the other end of the tunnel now."

A small circle of grey light appeared afar off. It grew bigger and bigger and the grey light appeared whiter. Soon it was as big as a door and the light was reflected on the damp sides of the tunnel. Then, almost before Jenny had time to see what was happening, the tunnel opened before them into a blaze of sunlight. The train rumbled out into the fresh sweet air again, between high embankments that became lower as they went along. The train jerked to a standstill. They had reached the end of the tunnel cable and another team of horses was waiting to be yoked to the train.

Mrs Mackay gave a great sigh of relief. "Thank goodness we're back into the daylight. Are you all there, children?" She counted them up. "Where's William?" she cried suddenly.

"On the gentleman's knee, Mother," Arabella said patiently. She was used to her mother missing one child out in the count.

"So he is! It's a mercy none of you fell off the train while we were in that terrible tunnel," Mrs Mackay declared.

"If any of them had, missus, it would have spoilt the record for the Innocent Railway," Mr Henderson told her.

"How's that?"

"We've never had an accident yet. That's why people call it the Innocent Railway."

They skirted a tremendous wall of rocky cliffs that fringed the great height of Arthur's Seat.

"Where are we?" James asked the driver.

"We've just come out from under Samson's Ribs. In a few minutes you'll pass the corner of Duddingston Loch."

"Why, we've sometimes fed the ducks there!" Jenny exclaimed in surprise. She was amazed that they were still so near home. They seemed to have been in that tunnel for hours.

The new team of horses was being yoked to the train.

Jenny turned round and caught Arabella smiling at her. She smiled back.

"Come and sit by me," Arabella invited her. "There's

more room here." She pushed Euphemia a little further along the seat. Jenny accepted the invitation and took the seat next to Arabella and behind James.

"Hold on to your seats now!" the train driver cried as he took hold of the reins again. "All aboard for Dalkeith!"

4

All Aboard for Dalkeith

The driver put the post-horn to his lips and sounded it, then clicked his tongue against his teeth and the obedient horses jerked forward.

"Why does the driver blow that horn?" William asked Mr Henderson.

"Because we're coming to the cross-roads at Dudding-ston. There's always someone waiting to get on the train there."

Sure enough, standing by the cross-roads was a neatly dressed young lady with two big round bonnet boxes on her arms.

"Och ay, there's the milliner who has a shop at Duddingston," Mr Henderson announced.

The handsome soldier sitting behind him leaned forward to look at the lady. "My, she's a bonnie wee lassie!" he exclaimed.

"Trust a soldier to have an eye for a bonnie lass," Mr Henderson remarked to Mrs Mackay.

The driver pulled up the horses and the train came to a halt. The soldier jumped down to help the pretty milliner with her boxes. "Up with you, ma'am. I'll lift up your boxes."

"Oh, thank you, sir. You'll be careful with them, now?" she asked anxiously.

"Oh ay, I will so!" the soldier promised. "Lift up your feet, folk, while I stow the boxes away under the seat. Take care ye don't ding them with your heels."

"The bonnets in those boxes are for ladies in Dalkeith who will be going to church with the Queen on Sunday," the little milliner told the passengers importantly.

"Those are awful heavy boxes for a wee lass like you to be carrying," the soldier told her.

"Ay, they fair make my arms ache," the milliner admitted.

"I've got a good strong arm. I'll give you a hand with them if you like, mistress."

The milliner hesitated.

"I'd take his offer, mistress," the driver advised. "He's a braw figure of a man in his red coat with the gold tassels on his shoulders. There'll be many a head turn after you both as you go through Dalkeith."

"Well, maybe I will," she agreed.

"I'm going to be one of the Queen's bodyguard in the Town Watch of Dalkeith as she goes through the

44

town. If you'll come with me when we've delivered the bonnets, mistress, I'll show you where you can stand to see the Queen well."

"Thank you, Sergeant. I'll take your kind offer." The milliner smiled at him sweetly.

"I thought you would!" the driver chuckled.

Mr Henderson was getting impatient. "Have you not got those boxes stowed away yet? If we're here much longer the time will have come for the Queen to go to church on Sunday!"

"But it's only *Friday* today," Jenny whispered to Arabella.

"Mr Henderson's just joking," Arabella whispered back.

"Come up! Come up!" the driver shouted to his horses, flicking the reins against their backs. Once more they jerked into action.

The milliner sat next to the soldier, but she did not look entirely happy. She kept sniffing the air with a look of disgust. At last she called out, "There's an awful smell in this carriage, driver!"

He turned round to her. "Nothing to worry about, miss! It's just coming from that cart-load of dung that we're pulling at the back of the train. It's going to a market-gardener near Dalkeith. It's a good healthy smell."

The milliner turned up her nose. "Disgusting, I call it!"

"Och! You'll not notice it much when we get moving faster. You'll see, the horses will go at a spanking pace. I wouldn't wonder but we do *eight* miles an hour!" the driver replied.

He gave a flick of his whip to the two horses and they broke into a trot that took the train forward at a quicker pace. As they were going downhill it almost seemed as though the train were pushing the horses. Mrs Mackay gave a cry of alarm and clutched Charlotte more closely. Jenny and Arabella held on to each other's arms.

"Oh, this is grand!" James cried and the driver urged the horses on faster still. For James his dream of the railway was coming true. At last he had been through the tunnel and he was really on the train on his way to Dalkeith. It was far, far better than he had even dreamed.

There was a shout from a side-road by the railway. "Wait, man, wait! I want to get on the train."

"There's a fish-wife running down that lane, driver," Mr Henderson cried.

"I can't pull up the horses now." The driver looked over his shoulder. "Och! It's just Maggie McClusky. She'll catch up with us round yon big bend at the passing place for the horses."

The train was now running on a single set of rails, but

round the bend of the railway was a loop line where the trains passed, one on its way to Dalkeith, one returning to Edinburgh.

Mr Henderson looked back. "Ay, there she is taking the short cut across the field, creel and all on her back, to head us off."

"Ay, she knows the railway takes yon big curve. Maggie McClusky aye runs across the field if she's too late at the lane end. I wouldn't wonder but she's at the passing place before we are," the driver said.

All the folk on the train turned their heads to watch Maggie McClusky fleeing across the field to get to the loop line.

"There she goes! Ay, she's half-way across the field! She'll get there in time. There! She's leaped the ditch!" excited voices exclaimed.

"Well done, Maggie McClusky!" Mr Henderson shouted. "You'll beat the train yet!"

When they reached the loop line the driver pulled his horses to a standstill and Maggie McClusky came puffing up to the train, shaking her fist.

"What for could ye no' wait for me, John Thomson, and me with a creel full of fish! I've half a mind to wipe you across the face with a herring!"

"Now, now, Mistress McClusky, calm yourself. Ye ken fine that I have to be at the loop line in time for the

other train to pass. You always catch up with us there."

Mrs McClusky was red-faced with anger and with running hard. "You could have taken time to wait a minute and pick me up."

"Ay, but it would have cost you the full fare from there. I only charge threepence from the passing place," John Thomson reminded her.

Mrs McClusky swallowed her anger. Threepence saved was not to be sneezed at. "Oh, well, I'll say no more about it. Move up, there, soldier, and you, mistress, and give me a seat." The fish-wife began to push her creel among the bonnet boxes under the seat.

The milliner looked annoyed. "Take care of those bonnet boxes!" she cried. "Mercy me! Am I to be plagued with the smell of fish now as well as dung?" She looked under the seat at the creel. "Oh, what's that thing crawling out of her creel?" she exclaimed in horror.

"Och! It's nothing but a crab!" Mrs McClusky said with a sneer at the milliner's fright.

"A crab! Oh dear! I feel quite faint!" The milliner pretended to go into a swoon.

"Lean on me, mistress! I'll not let the crab come near you," the soldier told her gallantly.

Mrs McClusky began to fill her little clay pipe with tobacco to have a smoke.

"No, no! Not that pipe-smoke along with the smell of dung and fish!" The little milliner looked quite sick.

"What's wrong with a sniff of tobacco? You'll not smell the dung so strong. My! There are some folk awful easy upset!" The fish-wife glared at her.

The soldier glared back. "Now, then, my good woman . . ." he was beginning but the driver had left his seat to settle the argument.

"Now, Mistress McClusky, you know right well there's a special open carriage at the back of the train where the fish-wives always sit. You can smoke your pipe there in peace. You'll oblige me by taking your proper place. Come along, now! I'll give you a hand with your creel."

Mrs McClusky knew when she was bested. "All right! All right! I'd like better to sit among my friends than where I'm not wanted." She rose and gave a sniff of disdain at the milliner and the soldier. The driver helped her down and carried her creel to the end of the train.

A number of people were waiting for the train to Dalkeith at the passing place.

"Oh, look!" Thomas cried. "There's a man with a drum round his neck and a trumpet in his hand. Is he going to get on the train?"

"Oh, ay, that's Hector McKee, the one man band," Mr Henderson told him. He called out, "Hullo, Hector! Are you coming to Dalkeith?"

"Ay, Mr Henderson. I'm off to entertain the crowds while I wait for the Queen."

"Maybe you'll give us a bit of a tune while we wait for the other train? I'll pass the hat round for you afterwards," Mr Henderson offered.

"Yes, I'll do that," Hector agreed gladly. He banged on his drum and tootled on his trumpet the tune of "The Bluebells of Scotland".

Mr Henderson obligingly passed round his hat.

James knew that the money in his pocket and Jenny's would not go very far. Though they each had a shilling, they had no coppers. They just could not afford to put a *whole shilling* in the hat if they were to pay their fares to Mrs Mackay when they reached Dalkeith. It would be dishonest if they did not. Then there would be the fare back home too and they might feel hungry in Dalkeith and need to buy a penny bun each. All the same, James did not want people to think they were mean. He turned round anxiously to Mr Henderson. "Please, sir, have you got change for a shilling?"

"Wait till you get to Dalkeith, laddie. I've not much change myself. Anyway, you can't spend it on the train."

"I . . . I wanted to put a penny in the hat for the man who played the drum," James faltered.

"Oh, we don't pass the hat to bairns. Besides, your mother has already put in some coins for all of you children." Mr Henderson took it for granted that James and Jenny belonged to Mrs Mackay too.

"Oh, but she isn't our mother!" James told him.

Mr Henderson looked astonished. "Then who are you with?"

"We're by ourselves," James said stoutly. "We're going to see the Queen."

Mr Henderson gave him a surprised look. Children in 1842 did not go on train journeys by themselves, even though the train was only drawn by horses. "Ah, but perhaps someone is meeting you in Dalkeith?" he asked.

James pretended not to hear him. He would not tell a lie but he did not want to be sent home again on the same train under the care of the driver. Mr Henderson was about to repeat his question but just then the train going in the opposite direction clanked into the loop line and took his attention. The second driver drew level with John Thomson's coach. "Good day to ye, John," he called.

"Good day, Bob. Your train's a bit late."

"Ay. Man, it's busy the day in Dalkeith. You'd

think the whole world there had turned up to see the Queen. Flags and bunting up everywhere and the streets are that thronged you can't turn round!"

"Ah, well, it's a grand day to see the Queen. Royal weather, right enough! How's your wife's rheumatism?" John enquired.

"Badly, man, badly. She fears there's a change coming in the weather, sure enough."

Mr Henderson was getting impatient at the delay while the two men chatted. "Man, John Thomson, if you don't move the train on soon, the change in the weather will be here!"

"Mercy on us, Mr Henderson, but you're an impatient man! Don't worry! I'll have you at Dalkeith in time to buy your oats at the market."

"Maybe, but not if you stop blethering here half the day!"

Other people were beginning to fret at the delay.

"I've got to take my place in the Dalkeith Town Guard," the soldier told the driver importantly.

"And I've got my bonnets to deliver before the Queen comes out from Dalkeith Palace, mind!" the milliner said in a high waspish voice.

From the coach at the back there came a shout. "What ails ye, John Thomson, that the train's no' moving? I want to get my fish sold today, not tomorrow."

"You'll be in plenty of time to call 'Fresh herring!', Mistress McClusky," the driver shouted back.

Even Mrs Mackay lent her voice to the chorus of complaints. "If we stand here much longer we'll be too late to see the Queen."

"My! You're all in a mighty hurry the day. Can a man not take time to exchange a few words with a friend? Well, I'll see you on the return journey, Bob." John Thomson lifted his reins again, but Bob wanted another word.

"Ay. When you get to Dalkeith will you call at my house and ask my wife for my piece of bread and cheese. I left it on the kitchen table."

Bob's "piece" was his sandwich lunch.

"I'll do that, Bob. Good-bye for now."

John Thomson blew on his horn again and the horses woke up from the little nap they had been having, heaved with their great shoulders, and away went the train in the direction of Dalkeith.

Arabella whispered to Jenny, "Are you truly by yourselves?"

Jenny nodded but put a finger to her lips and glanced towards Mr Henderson.

"Would you like to go along with us?" Arabella asked.

"But what would your mother say?"

"Oh, she won't bother. She'll never notice a couple more children if you stay beside me," Arabella giggled. Arabella was nearly twelve years old and felt quite grown up.

"It would be nice, but what about James?"

"Oh, he and Thomas are getting along together like a house on fire," Arabella smiled. Sure enough, James and Thomas were having a friendly chat about the horses.

The train rattled along, stopping every now and again to pick up passengers. That was the nice thing about the Innocent Railway. Whenever a passenger wanted to board the train, he just stood alongside the track and signalled to the driver who obligingly pulled up his horses.

From his high perch beside the driver James stared about him as the train skirted the Niddrie Mill. At New Hailes the railway took a sharp bend to the south through Whitehill. Now it was running among many coal-mines.

"What are those wheels on top of that wooden framework?" James asked the driver. "One wheel spins one way and the other wheel the opposite way."

"That's the winding gear for taking the miners down the coal-pits and bringing the coal up," the driver explained. "Have you never been on this railway before, laddie?"

James shook his head.

"Well, those coal-pits are really the reason why this railway was built, so as to haul the coal easily from the pits right into the heart of Edinburgh."

"Oh, yes, I can watch the coal trucks coming into the coal-yards at St Leonard's from my bedroom window," James told him.

The driver gave him a sharp look. "Live near St Leonard's, do you?"

It was on the tip of James's tongue to say "Gibraltar House" but he nipped off the words quickly and just nodded instead. The driver might begin asking awkward questions too. Just then a pedlar with a basket full of ribbons and bobbins of thread, pins and needles, bootlaces and skeins of mending wool, hailed the train from the track side.

"It should be a good day for you today at Dalkeith Market with all the folk coming to see the Queen," the driver told him as he boarded the train.

"Ay, that's why I'm going. Do you think folk will want to buy my penny favours?" The pedlar held up a bunch of knots of red, white and blue ribbon.

"Oh, ay. I'll have one off ye," the driver told him, pulling a penny from his pocket.

"What about the folk on the train? Will it be all right if I ask them to buy too?"

"Ay, you can do that. We all have to make a living," said the good-natured driver.

Business was brisk on the train. Mr Henderson bought a "favour" and Mrs Mackay bought seven "favours", one for herself and one for each of her children. This time she remembered how many children she had. Jenny looked wistful when she saw Arabella pinning on her knot of coloured ribbons. James turned round and caught her look. "Would you like one too?" he asked.

Jenny nodded. "But have we enough money?"

James did a rapid sum in his head. "Yes, we can manage it, but we may not be able to buy many buns when we reach Dalkeith." He brought out his shilling from his pocket. "Can you give me change?" he asked the pedlar.

"Ay, for sure," the pedlar said.

"Then two favours, please." When James put the tenpence change in his pocket it seemed a lot more money than his single shilling. (In 1842 there were twelve pence to a shilling.)

James and Jenny proudly pinned on the "favours".

The train went past the pig farms at Miller Hill. The prim little milliner turned up her prim little nose. "Oh, what a horrible smell!" she exclaimed.

"It's a right healthy country smell, mistress," the

driver told her, not bothering to turn round. "What should we do for our tasty bit of bacon if we hadn't got the pigs?"

The railway crossed three roads as they came towards Lugton on the outskirts of Dalkeith. The driver pulled up his horses.

"This is the best place for you folk to get off who want to see the Queen," he announced. "Climb the hill by that road in front of you and you'll find yourselves in the market place at Dalkeith."

There was a scramble to get off the train. James felt sorry to leave it and the friendly driver, but Jenny felt that *her* adventure was really beginning. She was going to see the Queen!

"Keep up with us," Arabella said over her shoulder to Jenny.

"Let's look at horses together," Thomas suggested to James as they stepped down from the train.

5

To See the Queen

At Dalkeith there was no station platform. Indeed there was no station! The train just stopped beside a farmhouse at the end of the lane up the hill. Here most of the passengers got down. The railway went on across the fields by Newbattle and Harden Green to the coalmines near Newtongrange where the coal trucks were filled, but not many passengers went so far.

As soon as Mrs Mackay got off the train James went to her and put sixpence into her hand. "Please, that's for our fares on the train and thank you for paying them," James said politely.

Mrs Mackay looked astonished. "But . . . but . . . I don't remember! Did I?"

"The driver thought we belonged to your family and he took our fares from you," James explained.

"Dear me! Well, you are an honest little lad. I'd never have known. Here, take it back again," she said generously, but James put his hands behind his back.

"No, no! Really, I *couldn't*. Thank you all the same, ma'am."

"Are you by yourselves?" Even Mrs Mackay looked surprised.

James nodded.

"Well, laddie, you're welcome to come along with us if there's no one meeting you," Mrs Mackay offered.

"We'll be pleased to do that, ma'am." James thanked her in his most grown-up manner.

Mrs Mackay and her family, along with James and Jenny, followed the crowd across the bridge over the river Esk, up the hill and into the very wide High Street near the old church. Here the street had widened into a market square set about with inns and shops. Dalkeith was famous for its market, for it stood in the midst of rich farm lands, famous for grain crops. Here, too, farm workers were hired for the year by the farmers. The harvest was just over and carts laden with sacks of oats had been rumbling into the market square from earliest light, waiting for the buyers from the many corn mills. Mr Henderson hurried ahead to inspect the grain and make his purchases to be sent to his mill. There he ground oats into oatmeal for porridge and oat-cakes.

Round the square were market stalls set out with onions, cabbages, kail, turnips, carrots, early potatoes and barrels of plums and pears. The fish-wives knelt on the cobbled pavements, their creels of fish before them and, as their customers chose their fish, they gutted it for them. There was an "egg-wife" with baskets of brown and white eggs and golden butter and a barefoot country lass beside her with a basket of water-cress and fresh-gathered mushrooms.

The gates of Dalkeith Palace park were at the very end of the market place. In the midst of the park was the Palace where the Queen was staying. That afternoon the young Queen Victoria was to pay a visit to Dalhousie Castle and to call also at Melville Castle on the return journey. Her carriage would be coming out from the gates of the park and into the very centre of Dalkeith. The large crowd which had gathered to see the Queen passed the time by walking round the market stalls. The baker's shop and the ginger-beer stalls did a merry business while the inns were crowded to the very doors. James and Jenny wandered about with the Mackay family from stall to stall. Jenny began to feel hungry. She wanted more than the bannock in her pocket.

"James, how much money have we got to spend?" she asked.

James did a hasty sum in his head. "I've got fourpence left. We'd better keep *your* shilling to pay our fares home. If the driver only charges us half-fare as he did last time, then we'll have sixpence left, but if we are by ourselves, he might charge us full-fare, so we'd better not spend your shilling. We can spend my fourpence, though."

The Mackay family began to feel hungry too and the little ones clamoured for a "piece" from their mother.

"We must find somewhere where I can sit down first," she said. "Oh dear! I'm beginning to feel quite faint."

Arabella knew just what to do. She rushed into a nearby shop. "Please, *please*, can you lend me a chair for my mother to sit down? She's feeling faint. She's got eight children with her!" Arabella included James and Jenny for good measure.

Mr Reid, the proprietor of the "Gentlemen's Tailoring Establishment", seized a chair and ran out into the street with it after Arabella.

"Here you are, ma'am!" he cried, thrusting the chair so suddenly under Mrs Mackay that she sat down very abruptly. Arabella was just in time to snatch Charlotte from her arms. Mrs Mackay fanned herself feebly with her handkerchief and Mr Reid rushed back into the shop to fetch her a glass of water. When he came back Arabella had gathered all the family about her mother and the young ones were sitting on the pavement at her feet.

"Oh, thank you, thank you, sir!" Mrs Mackay said in a feeble voice as she sipped the water.

"My! You *have* got a big family, ma'am!" Mr Reid said in surprise as he looked at the eight children. To him they seemed all very near the same age. "There'll be twins among them?"

"Yes," said Arabella quickly for her mother, and pointed to James and Jenny standing behind Mrs Mackay.

Mrs Mackay looked a bit startled to find twins had been wished upon her. "I . . . I don't think . . ." she was beginning but Arabella interrupted her hastily. "Don't worry, Mother! Just drink your water and you'll feel all right again in a minute."

Beyond giving James and Jenny a doubtful look as if she couldn't be sure whether they belonged to her or not, Mrs Mackay said nothing more, but sipped her water gratefully.

"All come to see the Queen, have you?" Mr Reid asked kindly. "Then just you stay where you are. You'll get a grand view from here. You're welcome to keep the chair till you go away, ma'am."

"Thank you, sir." Mrs Mackay replied, still sitting firmly as the Rock of Gibraltar, as she handed back the empty glass to him.

Once Mr Reid had disappeared inside the shop again, Arabella produced a large carpet bag which Thomas had been holding and handed it to her mother. Mrs Mackay rummaged inside it and brought out "baps" (bread rolls) sandwiched with jam and doled them out round the family. She would have handed baps to James and Jenny too but there was none left in the bag.

"Oh dear! Oh dear! I haven't enough!" she cried, looking rather distressed. Arabella was looking troubled too.

"I only put up seven baps," she told her mother. "I . . . I wasn't expecting company, but I'll give half my roll to Jenny and Thomas can give James half of his."

Thomas looked rather sadly at his roll. It looked rather small for two. James said hastily, "That's all right. We've got some money to buy buns. There's a baker's shop just over there. We'll go and get them now."

Thomas looked much happier. James seized Jenny by the hand and they ran along to the baker's shop.

"Two penny buns, please," James said. "The ones with pink sugar on the top."

"Oh, Miss Greig never lets us eat the buns with pink sugar," Jenny said doubtfully. "She says they're bad for our teeth."

"Miss Greig isn't here and *this time* we're going to please ourselves," James said firmly. "It's *our* money."

The baker's shop was also a dairy where milk was sold. It was in a big white bowl and the baker's wife used a large ladle to pour it into mugs at a penny a mug.

"Two mugs of milk, please," James said, offering the baker's wife another twopence. Somehow nothing had ever tasted so good and so refreshing as those buns and milk.

"That's all my shilling gone now," James told Jenny. "So hold on tight to your shilling and don't lose it. We don't want to have to walk all the way back from Dalkeith."

"You'd better take care of it in your trouser pocket," Jenny decided. "My pocket hangs by a ribbon from my waist and it's only meant for a handkerchief."

James slipped the shilling in his pocket beside the key of the back gate. They went back to join the Mackay family on the pavement to sit in the sun and wait for the Queen.

After a while the market people began to pack up their stalls. The market was over early on this particular day so as to make way for the Queen's carriage and because the stall-holders, as well as everybody else, wanted to see the Queen. When they had packed away their unsold goods they climbed on to their stalls and waited for the royal carriage. Even the men who had brought horses, cows and pigs, some of them still unsold, waited at the entrances to the side-roads.

It was rather a long wait and James and Thomas

began to be restless. "Let's go and look at the horses and pigs over there," Thomas suggested, pointing to some carts drawn up at the entrance to the yard of the Cross Keys Inn.

James was quite willing. They slipped away from the children around Mrs Mackay and, dodging behind the crowds, they reached the farm carts from which the grunting of pigs and the mooing of calves could be heard. The farm horses stood there patiently, nodding their heads in the warm sun, ready harnessed to move away once the Queen had passed by.

All eyes were fixed on the gates to the Palace park. Inside the park there were smaller crowds of the tenants and workers and their families on the Duke of Buccleuch's estate, waiting too to wave to the Queen. Just before four o'clock a cheer went up from them. "The Queen's coming! She's in her carriage now."

Their shouts were echoed by the crowds outside the gate. The Duke's menservants came out to clear the way for the Queen's carriage and the soldiers in the Dalkeith Town Watch pushed the crowds back to the pavements. Even James and Thomas forgot about the horses.

"Let's climb on to this cart. We'll have a grand view from there," Thomas said.

James looked doubtfully at the cart. "It's got pigs in it."

"They'll no' harm you! Come on, feartie!"

Thomas climbed up and James did not want to be thought afraid so he climbed up after Thomas and they both sat on the front ledge of the cart.

A wave of cheering swept across the square. The Queen's carriage emerged from the gate and there was Queen Victoria sitting up in it very straight and proper, smiling at the cheers of the people. Beside her was her husband, Prince Albert. They made a very handsome young couple. The cheering grew louder as the Queen bowed graciously to each side and the Prince raised his hand in a salute.

From the pavement at the front of the crowd the Mackay family had a very good view. Mrs Mackay stood up and lifted Charlotte on to her chair to see better. She was overcome with delight.

"Oh, there's the Queen! My! Doesn't she look grand with those footmen in red and gold coats and white breeches perched up behind the carriage. Look! She's bowing towards us now." Mrs Mackay waved her handkerchief wildly at the Queen.

The prim little milliner was standing just beside Mrs Mackay. "Oh, isn't the Queen sweet in that pink silk bonnet and wine-coloured silk gown?"

"Ay, she's right bonnie! And what a handsome man the Prince is, to be sure!" Mrs Mackay quickly agreed.

"Hold up Sarah so she can see better, Arabella."

It was just at that moment that Arabella missed Thomas!

Jenny's eyes were fixed on the Queen. At last she was seeing her! Her dream was coming true, and the Queen was actually looking towards *her*, Jenny! As the Queen saw the eager face of the little girl she smiled. Jenny smiled back and dropped a little curtsey as she stood at the edge of the pavement. The Queen had smiled at her, Jenny! Jenny's heart thumped with joy. Just then Arabella jogged her elbow. "Where are Thomas and James? I can't see them anywhere."

Jenny came back to earth with a bump. "James? No, no! Where are they?" A sick feeling of fright overcame her. Without James she was lost! Besides, he had her shilling for her fare home.

Arabella was tugging at Mrs Mackay's sleeve. "Mamma! Mamma! Where's Thomas?"

Mrs Mackay was still watching the royal carriage move away. "There's to be a grand ball at Dalkeith Palace tonight. Oh, I wish I could be there to see the Queen in her diamond tiara and satin gown!" she sighed. Arabella tugged harder at her sleeve. "What's the matter, Arabella?" she asked crossly.

"Thomas isn't here, Mamma. I can't see him anywhere in the crowd. He's lost!"

Mrs Mackay came suddenly to herself. "What's that, Arabella?" she snapped.

"Thomas! He was standing just by me and now I can't see him anywhere. Jenny's lost James too."

Jenny was looking distressed and tearful. "How will I get home without James?" she sobbed.

"Oh dear! Oh dear! However shall we find them in all this throng? Mercy me, what a thing to happen! Oh, what shall I do?" Mrs Mackay wailed, feeling helpless. "Oh, why didn't you keep hold of his hand, Arabella?"

"I couldn't, Mother. I was holding up Sarah," Arabella pointed out.

The milliner took hold of Mrs Mackay's arm. "What's the matter? Is it the little boy you called Thomas?"

"Yes, yes! Can you see him?"

Crowds of people were sweeping past them in the wake of the Queen's carriage, hoping to get another glimpse of her.

"He ran across the road with the other lad," the milliner told Mrs Mackay. "Look, they're both standing on top of that farm cart."

Sure enough, the boys were both standing perilously on the front ledge of the pig cart the better to see the Queen go by.

"Come down! Come down at once, Thomas! At once, or I'll spank you!" Mrs Mackay shouted, but her cries could not be heard above all the cheering. Just then the Dalkeith Town Band burst into a blare of martial music.

The boys had their backs to the pigs. One of them was startled by the sudden noise of the trumpets. He rushed to the front of the cart and put his forelegs up between Thomas's feet and pushed Thomas just behind the knees with his snout. Thomas toppled backwards among the pigs! He let out a yell of terror. He was in danger of being trampled on by the pigs as he lay flat on his back. James bravely jumped down into the cart to ward off the pigs and help Thomas to rise.

Mrs Mackay saw Thomas fall and shrieked. "Oh! He's fallen among the pigs. They'll kill him! Oh, just think of the state his clothes will be in! Oh, I'm going to faint!"

Whenever a crisis arose Mrs Mackay always felt faint. Arabella, as usual, had to cope with things.

"Please help my mother into the shop," she asked the milliner. "The rest of you children stand here and don't you dare move! Come along, Jenny! We'll get hold of those boys."

The two girls pushed their way through the crowd to the cart. When they got there the farmer was

already lifting down a very dirty Thomas who was wailing loudly. James, rather white-faced, and also dirty, climbed down himself. He, too, had slipped and fallen just as the farmer pushed away the pigs.

"Oh, just look at you!" Arabella scolded Thomas. "You're filthy! Whatever will Mamma say when she sees your clothes?"

Jenny was shocked too when she looked at her twin, but all she could say was "Oh, James, are you hurt?"

James shook his head, looking rather dazed and ashamed. He looked ruefully at the knees of his breeches and at his hands. Jenny seized a piece of bunting that had been pulled off some of the decorations and helped him to wipe the worst of the dirt off his hands and knees.

Arabella marched Thomas across the street, holding him at arms' length and the twins followed meekly after her.

Mrs Mackay emerged from the shop along with the milliner and Mr Reid when they saw the children cross the road to them. Mrs Mackay nearly had another fainting fit when she saw the state Thomas was in. She closed her eyes in horror and rocked back on her heels. "Oh, give me my smelling-salts!" she cried. Arabella dived into the carpet bag and brought out the smelling-salts and the milliner held them to Mrs Mackay's nose. She held them so close that they made Mrs Mackay sneeze and choke, and she recovered herself sharply. She looked at Thomas in disgust. "If you were not so filthy I'd spank you here and now!" she declared in wrath. Thomas set up another wail.

"Perhaps we'd better get home now, Mamma," Arabella said sensibly.

"Yes, I think we'd better go too," Jenny agreed. For once James made no objection but nodded unhappily.

The subdued little party set off for the railway at the foot of the hill, Arabella leading them and carrying Charlotte. Mrs Mackay marched Thomas in front of her, wrinkling her nose in disgust, and uttering threats of what would happen when she got him home. James and Jenny tailed on behind, Jenny looking rather forlorn at this sad ending to her joy in seeing the Queen. Now she and James must go home and what would happen to them when they got there? Jenny gave an unhappy shiver.

6

Return Home

Very tired, the twins and the Mackays waited at the foot of the hill for the train to take them back to Edinburgh. Soon they heard the clop-clop of the horses' hoofs and the rattle of the wheels as the train came round the bend. John Thomson was driving the horses again. Mr Henderson was on the train too. He gave Mrs Mackay and the children a hand up on to the coach.

"Well, have you bairns had a good day?" he asked.

"Very nice, thank you," Jenny replied politely. She was followed by James who hung his head and hoped Mr Henderson would not notice the stains on the knees of his breeches. Mrs Mackay kept a firm hold on the back of Thomas's collar, though she held him at arms' length.

James settled himself in the front seat beside the driver and made room for Thomas to sit beside him but Mrs Mackay still held on tightly.

"Please, I want to sit beside the driver and watch the horses, Mamma," Thomas begged.

"You've been a bad boy and you'll sit beside *me*," his mother told him.

"But I wanted to watch the horses!" Thomas's voice rose to a wail.

"Be quiet, or it's a sound whipping and bread and water you'll get for your supper, my lad!" Mrs Mackay warned him.

"Why, what's the laddie done?" the driver asked.

"He ran away from us all and went and stood on a cart full of pigs so he could see the Queen and he fell among the pigs," Arabella explained.

The driver tried to keep a straight face. "And did you see the Queen, laddie?" he asked.

Thomas hesitated. "Well . . . I saw the Queen's *horses*. They were grand! They were fine light-grey ones, but I like better the horses that pull this train."

The driver was pleased. "Good for you, my boy!"

"The Queen's *horses*, indeed!" Mrs Mackay sniffed. "Did you not see the Queen?"

"The Queen? Which lady was she?" Thomas asked vaguely.

"Why! She was sitting in the carriage behind the grey horses, silly!" Arabella told him.

"Oh, yon wee woman! Was she the Queen?" Thomas sounded surprised.

"And to think I took you all the way to Dalkeith to

see the Queen and all you could look at were the horses!" Mrs Mackay exclaimed, sorely vexed.

"But I *did* see her," Thomas protested, "but I didn't know she was the Queen because she wasn't wearing a crown. She was just wearing a bonnet and it wasn't as smart as yours, Mamma."

The folk on the coach all laughed but Mrs Mackay was secretly pleased, though she cried, "What a thing to say, to be sure!"

"Please, Mamma, I want to sit beside James and the driver and watch the horses," Thomas begged again.

"You'd better let him come and sit beside the other little lad. There's a kind of smell of pigs about them both, ye ken. They're better on the front seat with me than mixing with the other passengers," John Thomson suggested.

Mrs Mackay gave in. "Very well, then, Thomas, but see you behave yourself! Arabella, you sit behind him to keep an eye on him."

Arabella and Jenny sat behind the two boys, though they kept sniffing and giggling and pretending to pull faces of disgust at their brothers. Mr Henderson sat on the seat behind the driver too.

"All aboard?" John Thomson shouted, taking a careful look up the hill to make sure no passengers were running for the train. Sure enough, Maggie McClusky was late as usual and shouting for him to wait for her! Driver Thomson obligingly waited this time. "You've just made it, mistress," he told her. "Into the last coach, please."

Mrs McClusky was too puffed to argue and got into the last coach without a word.

"Right! Now we'll be off!" Driver Thomson announced. He sounded his post-horn. "Come up, Bonnie! Come up, Turk!" He clicked his tongue at the horses, shook the reins and obediently they heaved their shoulders and plodded on, dragging the train along the rails.

Soon they were moving between fields of ripened oats that farmers were beginning to harvest. Mr Henderson looked at the crops with a keen eye. "Farmer Douglas has a bonnie crop there, John," he remarked.

"Och aye, he's done well with his grain this year. He's sold a lot of it to the flour mills at Dalkeith," the driver replied.

"That's what I like about this railway. You can hear what's going on in the countryside and you can watch the crops growing," Mr Henderson said.

"No, surely we don't go as slowly as all that!" the driver laughed. "Though it's true we've got instructions not to let our horses crop the grass by the railway side."

Mr Henderson laughed too. "At least we're not being

rushed about by these new-fangled whistling screaming locomotive engines, letting off steam whistles fit to deafen you, such as they've got in Glasgow now."

"True, sir! But there's a railway planned between Edinburgh and Berwick with trains drawn by those steam-engines," the driver told him. "The time will come, you'll see, when they'll take over this railway for steam trains too."

"Long may the day be before that happens!" Mr Henderson remarked. "I like to have time to look around as I go along, and call 'Good-day' to the folk I see on the road."

"The day may come sooner than you think. Then I'll lose my job, for I know nothing about driving steam-engines, only horses."

Thomas muttered sleepily, "I like the horses."

"So do I!" James echoed.

"The laddies are right, even though they're half-asleep," Mr Henderson laughed. "I like the horses too and the Innocent Railway. It's a friendly kind of railway."

The horses jogged along steadily and the Mackay family became drowsy and quiet and even Mrs Mackay's head began to nod to the sound of the clop-clop of the horses' hoofs. Only Arabella stayed awake, keeping an eye on the rest of the family. Jenny's head

lolled against her shoulder and Arabella put a protecting arm round her. James made himself stay awake too, determined not to miss a minute of his return journey on his beloved railway.

There was a short stop at the Niddrie cross-roads to let some passengers off, then the horses toiled upwards past Duddingston. At last they reached the entrance to the long sloping tunnel. They stopped without any command from John Thomson for this was where they always stopped while they were unyoked from the train. It was a welcome rest.

Most of the sleepy passengers woke up as the wire rope was attached to the foremost carriage. The driver lighted his lantern. Then began the long haul into the tunnel and up the slope towards St Leonard's and Edinburgh again.

James took a deep breath of joy as the slimy walls of the tunnel enclosed him. This was adventure! Jenny stirred restlessly and longed for the blink of daylight to appear at the other end of the tunnel. Arabella slipped her arm into Jenny's as if she knew how she was feeling. At last they came up the ramp into daylight and into the great coal-depot of St Leonard's with all its side-rails fanning out to the different coal-yards. Here another team of horses waited to be yoked on to take the passengers to the "station" at the gates at the far end of the yard. It was then that James knew with a cold shock that the adventure was over! He turned to Jenny and he could tell from her face that she knew it too.

At the station they scrambled down from the train.

"Good-bye," James said to the kind driver. "I did like the horses."

"Aye, they're fine friendly beasts," the driver said warmly.

"I liked the horses too," Thomas said. He and James grinned at each other.

"Come and ride with us again another time," the driver invited them.

Arabella and Jenny were parting from each other rather sadly. "I wish I could see you again," Jenny said.

"Where do you live?" Arabella asked.

Jenny pointed to Gibraltar House with its back windows overlooking the station yard.

"Is that the back of the house?"

"Yes."

"And the front of it looks out on the Queen's Park and Arthur's Seat?"

"Yes, it does." Jenny nodded.

"I often wheel Charlotte out in the park. We live in Rankeillor Street. It's quite near. I'll look out for you in the park," Arabella suggested.

"But we're not allowed out alone," Jenny said

miserably. "Miss Greig is always with us. Today we . . . we ran away from home and after today they won't ever allow us to go out without Miss Greig." Jenny's lip quivered.

Arabella seemed to understand. "Cheer up!" she said. "We can *wave* to each other. Miss Greig can't stop you waving from your window, and Miss Greig won't *always* be with you. We shall find a way someday to be friends, you'll see."

Arabella sounded so certain that Jenny knew she was right and she felt less unhappy. She and James said goodbye to the Mackays and they made their way towards the back door in the garden wall of their house. They were very quiet as they crossed the railway yard. As they reached the other side James said, "We'll be in for it now, Jenny."

No need to explain to Jenny what "it" was! "We'll be punished, won't we?" Jenny asked miserably.

"Yes, I expect so, unless a miracle happens." James sounded unhappy too. "I got you into this, Jenny. I'll take the blame."

"No, no! We were *both* in it," Jenny told him. "Anyway I saw the Queen and I made friends with Arabella."

"And *I* went on the railway and went down the tunnel." James brightened up. "Even though they punish us, they can't take *that* from us. Today will always be something to remember." He squared his shoulders and marched towards the door, feeling in his pocket for the key. As he slipped it into the lock he turned to Jenny. "We'd better go straight upstairs and tell the truth and get it over, only a miracle could save us."

Jenny gave an unhappy shiver.

"It's all right. Father won't spank you because you're a girl," James tried to comfort her.

"It's just as bad if he spanks you. I'm going to pray for a miracle to happen." Jenny closed her eyes tightly in prayer.

"You'd better open your eyes or you'll fall up the steps," James managed to giggle at her.

He pushed open the garden gate and they went up the steps.

7

The Miracle

James opened the house door very quietly and they crept up the cellar steps but, as they passed the kitchen door, it suddenly opened. There was Maggie!

"Where have you been?" she demanded. "I've been hunting high and low for you. You're to go straight up to your father in his study." Then she saw how dirty James's breeches were at the knees. "Goodness! Where have you been to get like that? You'd better go and change your breeches first and wash yourself, but be quick about it. Hurry up! You don't want to get your father angry today of all days."

As they stumbled up the stairs James whispered grimly to Jenny, "I should think he'd be angry whether it's today or any other day."

James changed speedily into a clean pair of breeches while Jenny brushed her hair, then they both crept from their attics and downstairs to the study door. James tapped gently on it and they took a deep breath.

"Come in!" their father called.

He was busy writing letters when the twins slipped

nervously round the door. To their astonishment he looked up with a *smile*!

"Oh, there you are! Come with me. I've something to show you."

Mystified, the twins followed him from the room. He led them to their mother's bedroom, opened the door gently and put his finger to his lips. "Quiet now!" he warned them. They tiptoed after him. There was Mother, in bed, but looking radiant and smiling too. A strange lady in a nurse's cap and apron, was just lifting a cup of beef-tea to her lips. The lady smiled at the twins too. It was then that they both noticed the cradle standing by the bed.

"Come and look at your new little brother. He came today," their father said. He gently lifted back the coverlet of the cradle but the baby was awake. It seemed to the twins that he looked at them solemnly with his big blue eyes, but he did not cry.

Jenny took a big breath. "Oh, isn't he wonderful?" she exclaimed, looking at James. "He's a *miracle*."

"He's *our* miracle!" James agreed in a low voice.

Father heard what they said and he looked pleased. "Every new baby is a miracle. But come and speak to your mother now."

"You like your new brother?" she asked.

The twins nodded happily.

"And what have you done with yourselves today? You've been very quiet."

This was the question they had been dreading but Jenny answered truthfully, "We went to see the Queen."

To her surprise her mother did not ask *where* they had seen the Queen. All she said was "What was she like?"

"She was wearing a dark red silk gown and a pink bonnet with lace. She was quite pretty."

James chimed in with, "But she wasn't nearly as pretty as you are, Mamma." He meant what he said for he had suddenly realized how beautiful his mother was. His answer seemed to please his parents for they both smiled at each other.

"Have you had your teas yet?" Father asked. The twins shook their heads.

"Then run downstairs now and ask Maggie to give you some. She'll have been too busy to bother up till now."

When Maggie brought their tea to the school-room she asked, "Where did you get to all on your own today without Miss Greig?"

"Oh, round and about," James said vaguely.

Jenny put a sudden question, "What did Miss Greig think of the new baby?"

Maggie threw her a sharp glance. "Miss Greig doesn't know about him. She didn't come today. She sent word she'd a bad headache. But how is it you didn't know that?"

"No one told us," James said quite truthfully.

"Oh, well, maybe it was forgotten in the stramash of the baby arriving."

A bell tinkled down in the kitchen. "Mercy me! It'll be that nurse ringing again! She's aye wanting something fetched up. I'll have climbed the stairs as high as the top of Arthur's Seat by the time the day is ended!" Maggie grumbled as she disappeared with the streamers of her white cap flying.

For a few minutes there was silence in the schoolroom as the twins made up for the meal they had missed, then Jenny said quietly, "So Miss Greig never came today!"

James looked thoughtful. "No. And everybody was so busy with the new baby coming that no one knows we went out all day by ourselves."

"Mother can't have known that Miss Greig wasn't here. She must think we went with Miss Greig to see the Queen."

"So no one need ever know about our big adventure," James replied, but both twins looked at each other rather guiltily. They went on with their tea in silence, then James got to his feet. "I can't eat another mouthful. I've *got* to go upstairs to tell Father."

"Are you going to tell him about the railway?"

"Yes, but you don't need to come with me."

"You're not going alone. *I* shall come too. We've always been in everything together," Jenny said with determination, though she looked a little fearful.

They paused for a moment outside the door of their father's study. Jenny held back a little but James knocked on the door and they both plunged into the room. Mr Murray looked up in surprise from his letter-writing.

"Please, Father, may we talk to you? It's something we've *got* to tell you . . . something we've done," James stammered. "But it was my fault, really, not Jenny's. It was *my* idea, so you won't punish her, will you?"

"But I was in it too," Jenny said in a trembling little voice.

Mr Murray put down his pen. He knew the twins were in real distress. "Suppose you come over here and tell me all about it," he said quietly.

"It . . . it was because I wanted to go on the Innocent Railway and Jenny wanted to see the Queen and it was no use asking Miss Greig," James began and out tumbled the whole story of their runaway adventure, not forgetting the Mackays and the pigs! At the end of it there was silence for a minute, then Mr Murray asked a question. "Are you sorry you went?"

James felt he had to tell the truth. "N . . . no, Father. I . . . I liked the Innocent Railway and the horses so much."

"And you, Jenny?" Mr Murray turned to her.

"I wanted to see the Queen and I *did* see her," Jenny said stoutly. "And I liked Arabella too and I wish I could have her for a friend."

Mr Murray fiddled with his pen for a moment, then he said, "You know your mother might have been very worried if she had known you were missing?"

The twins looked troubled and ashamed and James said in a low voice, "Yes, we are sorry about *that*, Father."

Jenny added, "It was a good thing she didn't know and our baby brother came just like a miracle when he did."

There was a hint of a smile in Mr Murray's eyes. "You are both getting older and I suppose you will sometimes want to go out by yourselves, but I want you to promise me that you will never go out by yourselves again without first telling us where you are going."

"Yes, yes. We'll promise," the twins said.

"Then we'll say no more about it this time."

Jenny let out a big sigh of relief and turned towards the door, thinking they were dismissed, but James stood still, looking up at his father.

"Father, may I ask you a question?"

"Yes, James. What is it?"

"Why is the railway called the *Innocent* Railway?"

"Because in all the years it has been running there has never been an accident on it nor a single life lost because of it. It has been *innocent* of injury to anyone." Mr Murray seemed lost in thought for a minute. "Perhaps it's because there's something unspoilt and childlike about it: a railway that has never grown up. What was it you liked about it so much, James?"

"The horses," James answered promptly. "I liked the tunnel too, but the horses most of all." A troubled look crossed his face. "Father, will there always be horses on the Innocent Railway?"

"Why do you ask, James?"

"Because Mr Thomson, the driver, was telling a passenger that the train might someday be pulled by steam-engines that moved and there'd be no use for horses then and he'd lose his job. It isn't true, is it?"

Mr Murray gave James an understanding look. "The driver was telling the truth, James. A new railway is being built from Berwick-on-Tweed to Edinburgh, to link up with the new railway to London. In a year or two people will be able to go right from Edinburgh to London in trains pulled by steam locomotives and the journey will probably only take a day."

"Then what will happen to the Innocent Railway and the horses?" James asked.

"The horses will probably go to work on the farms and the new North British Railway will take over the railroad tracks between here and Dalkeith to add to its own railway system."

"No, no!" James cried, not far from tears. "I don't want it to happen. I want the Innocent Railway and the horses to be there always."

Mr Murray shook his head a little sadly. "The world can't stand still, James. Even you are growing up and want to do things differently. Things have to change. That's *progress*. Maybe when you grow up you'll learn to love the steam-engines and the new railways too. But cheer up! It'll be a few years yet before the changes come and you'll have plenty of chances to go on the Innocent Railway again. And, whatever happens, you'll always be able to remember today and your first journey on it. Was it good?"

"It was *very* good," James said. He and his father looked at each other with warm understanding.

"You both must be tired. It's been a long day for all of us. What about an early bed?"

The twins nodded. All at once they did feel tired. They slipped along to the bedroom and whispered good-night to their mother and took another peep at their new brother. The "miracle" was fast asleep.

In her bedroom Jenny leaned out of the window and looked at Arthur's Seat, shining and dappled in the light of the sunset reflected on it from the west. It looked mysterious and lovely, brooding over the city at its feet. Jenny heaved a big sigh of content. "I don't ever want to leave you, *my* mountain," she whispered. "Someday I shall climb you again with Arabella."

Before he got into bed James opened his window and looked out over the railway yard. The sunset glow was upon it, turning its dust into a golden haze. The last train had come up from the tunnel and the patient horses were hauling it over to the station. James watched them for a minute or two. "I shan't ever forget you, Innocent Railway," he promised quietly.

Then he closed the window.

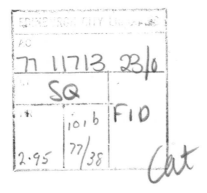